Adapted by Hollis James

Based on the teleplay "Ready, Race, Rescue!" by Andy Guerdat and Steve Sullivan

Illustrated by MJ Illustrations

A Random House PICTUREBACK® Book

Random House 🏠 New York

rhcbooks.com

ISBN 978-0-593-12133-7

MANUFACTURED IN CHINA

10 9 8 7 6 5 4 3 2

It was the day of the Adventure Bay 500, a very important car race. All the best racers were there: Riff Rockinbock, Lionel Lightspeed, Willy Widewheels Jr., and the mighty Whoosh! The PAW Patrol was excited to be the pit crew.

"Marshall, you must be the Whoosh's biggest fan-pup ever," said Skye.

"I am," said Marshall. "I've seen every one of his races!"

Just then, the Cheetah screeched up to the starting line.
She was Mayor Humdinger's niece and a very sneaky racer.
"Eat my dust, pups!" she said when the qualifying race
began.

"And they're off—except for the Whoosh!" said Ron Rapidfire, the announcer. "He seems to be stuck at the starting line."

Mayor Humdinger had ordered his Kitten Catastrophe Crew to glue the Whoosh's tires to the track!

"I'm ready to do a *ruff-ruff* repair!" said Marshall, who had his hydroblaster.

"I've got lots more dirty tricks," said the Cheetah, pushing a button in her car. A spear came out of her wheel and punctured Lionel Lightspeed's tire!

"Don't worry, Lionel," said Ryder. "The pit-crew pups will get you back in the race!"

The PAW Patrol raced to the rescue in their brand-new Mobile Pit Stop.

Riff's speakers were blasting loud music as he caught up to the Cheetah. "I've got a new song for you," said the Cheetah. "It's called 'The Foggy Bottom Blues.'"

She pushed a button, and a blue fog immediately sprayed from her car. Both Willy and Riff crashed!

The Mobile Pit Crew was quickly on the scene.
"Wow, the pit-crew pups have had their paws full today!"
declared Ron Rapidfire.

Cheetah pushed another button, and another dirty trick took the Whoosh out of the race!

"Whoosh, are you okay?" asked Marshall.

"I must have banged my arm," said the Whoosh. "I can't drive like this—but *you* can drive, Marshall."

Marshall couldn't say no to his favorite driver, so he took the Whoosh's place in the next race. He zoomed along the track, screeching around the turns.

"Marshall has taken the lead as they head for the finish line!" announced Ron Rapidfire.

"That's pup's finished, all right," said the Cheetah. "Now to slingshot to victory. See ya!"

With that, the Cheetah fired a rope at Marshall's car, which pulled him back while she zoomed ahead of him. Marshall's car went spinning!

"And the winner of the Adventure Bay 500 is . . . the Cheetah!" said Ron. There was one more race left—the Road Rally Championship.

The Whoosh's arm wouldn't be better in time for the championship, so he trained Marshall to take his place. He taught the pup how to drift, slide, and glide.

"I've got a very serious and important racing tip for you," said the Whoosh. "Smile, buddy! Racing is fun."

"I can definitely do that!" said Marshall.

In the Cheetah's hideout, the Humdingers were making plans.

"The Whoosh is training that pup to race against you," said Mayor Humdinger.

The Cheetah thought for a moment. "We need to upgrade my race car . . . by taking the best parts from everyone else's!"

Mayor Humdinger used his blimp to steal the other drivers' cars.

He even snatched up the Whoosh so he couldn't coach Marshall!

"This rescue has a need for speed!" Ryder declared.
He used the Mobile Pit Stop to jazz up all the pups' rescue vehicles.
Engines revved and roared as the PAW Patrol raced to the rescue!

Back at the track, it was time for the championship race. The Cheetah rolled up in her racer, which had been turbocharged with all the best parts from the stolen cars.

"There's no one to challenge the Cheetah!" exclaimed Mayor Goodway.

"I guess that means I win," said the Cheetah.

Just then, Marshall rolled up in his super-rescue car.

"I'm racing for Team Whoosh!" he declared. But then he radioed Ryder. "Have you rescued the Whoosh yet? I could really use his coaching about now."

"We're still after him, Marshall," Ryder replied. "Hang in there!"

"Ready, set, race!" said Mayor Goodway, and the cars sped off!

Meanwhile, the rest of the pups worked together to save the Whoosh. Skye caught Mayor Humdinger's blimp in her turbojet.

Rocky built a ramp . . .

. . . which Chase used to launch himself midair to free the Whoosh.

The Whoosh fell into the bay, where Zuma picked him up!

The race went on. The Cheetah tried her slingshot move again. Marshall began to spin out of control, just like before. But then he remembered what the Whoosh had taught him. He stayed calm and steered through the spin.

"Way to go, Marshall!" said a familiar voice through Marshall's Pup Tag.

"Whoosh!" exclaimed Marshall. "You're back!"

"Ryder and the pups saved me," said the Whoosh. "But no one needs to save you. You can win this race all on your own."

"I can!" said Marshall. "I'll try to drift, slide, and glide, just like you taught me."

Marshall sped toward the finish line.

He won the race!

"This championship really belongs to the Whoosh," Marshall declared. "I couldn't have won it without him."

"Thanks," said the Whoosh, "but you won on your own, with the true heart of a racer!"

Mayor Goodway presented Marshall with a trophy, and everyone cheered!